Let's Look at the Seasons

Wintertime

By Ann Schweninger

VIKING

The art was prepared with graphite pencil, colored
pencil, and watercolor paint on Arches 90-pound
cold-press watercolor paper.

VIKING
Published by the Penguin Group
Viking Penguin, a division of Penguin Books USA Inc.,
375 Hudson Street, New York, New York 10014 U.S.A.
Penguin Books Ltd, 27 Wrights Lane, London W8 5TZ, England
Penguin Books Australia Ltd, Ringwood, Victoria, Australia
Penguin Books Canada Ltd, 2801 John Street, Markham, Ontario, Canada L3R 1B4
Penguin Books (N.Z.) Ltd, 182–190 Wairau Road, Auckland 10, New Zealand

Penguin Books Ltd, Registered Offices: Harmondsworth, Middlesex, England

First published in 1990 by Viking Penguin, a division of Penguin Books USA Inc.
10 9 8 7 6 5 4 3 2 1
Copyright © Ann Schweninger, 1990
All rights reserved

Library of Congress Cataloging in Publication Data
Schweninger, Ann.   Wintertime
by Ann Schweninger.   p.   cm.
Summary: A dog family explores the changes that happen
in nature during the winter.
ISBN 0-670-83420-3
[1. Winter—Fiction   2. Nature—Fiction.   3. Dogs—Fiction.]   I. Title.
PZ7.S41263Wi 1990   [E]—dc20   90-12261

Printed in Japan
Set in Cheltenham Book

For Barbara Hennessy and Deborah Brodie

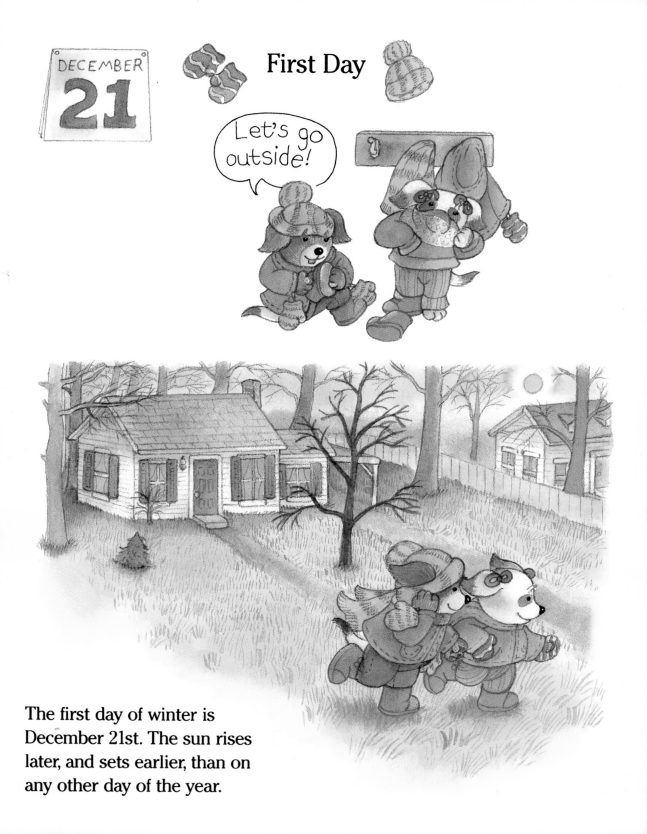

First Day

The first day of winter is December 21st. The sun rises later, and sets earlier, than on any other day of the year.

Early Winter

Winter is the coldest time of year.
The earth is farthest away from the
warmth of the sun.

Rabbits live in old burrows dug by
woodchucks or skunks. They eat
twigs and buds.

Chipmunks dig their own little tun-
nels to live in and store seeds for
food.

Squirrels live in nests in hollow
trees. They bury nuts in the ground,
to dig up when they are hungry.

A woodchuck closes the opening to
its burrow to keep out the cold air.
The woodchuck, sometimes called a
groundhog, sleeps all winter.

Frost and Ice

When the temperature falls below 32°, dew and moisture become frost. Water freezes and turns to ice.

Sometimes ice melts, drips, and freezes again. Then icicles are made.

Have you heard of Jack Frost? Stories tell us that he crosses the land, covering it with frost.

Animals in Winter

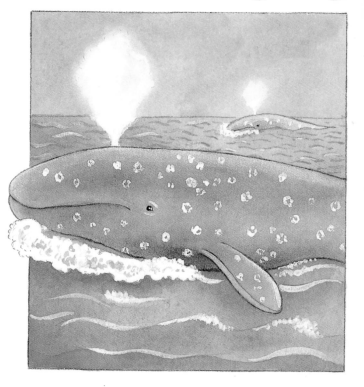

During winter some animals go to warmer places where there is plenty of food.

California gray whales migrate. So do monarch butterflies.

Other animals sleep all winter, usually underground or inside a cave.

Grizzly bears hibernate all winter. So do bats, turtles, and snails.

Some animals stay on through the cold winter.

Animals with fur grow thick long coats to stay warm.
Deer grow warm coats. So do raccoons and foxes.
Birds fluff their feathers to stay warm.

Making a Bird Feeder

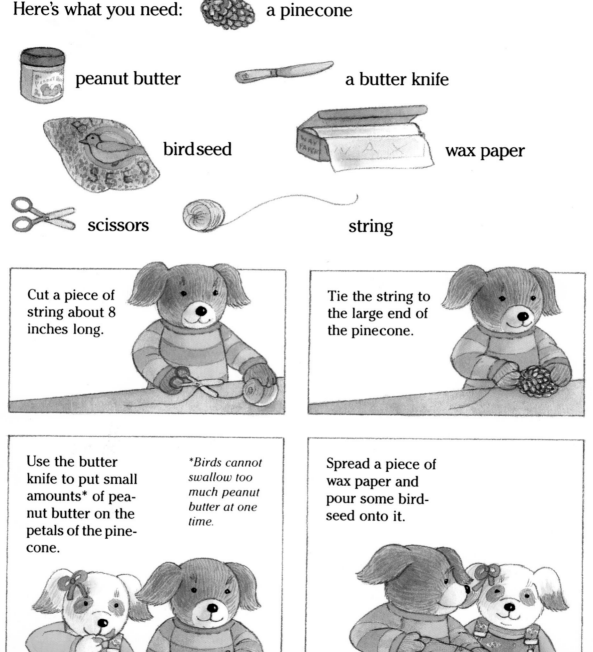

Here's what you need: a pinecone

peanut butter

a butter knife

birdseed

wax paper

scissors

string

Cut a piece of string about 8 inches long.

Tie the string to the large end of the pinecone.

Use the butter knife to put small amounts* of peanut butter on the petals of the pinecone.

*Birds cannot swallow too much peanut butter at one time.

Spread a piece of wax paper and pour some birdseed onto it.

Roll the pine-
cone in the seed.

Hang it up where
wild birds will
find it.

Once you begin to feed wild
birds, they count on you, so
please keep feeding them all
through the winter.

Winter Tree

During winter, a tree rests. Its leaves have fallen and sap has left the branches.

The branches have winter buds. The buds are made of tiny folded leaves.

Even the roots are resting. They do not grow during the winter.

Tough scales protect the outside of the buds.

Happy New Year!

 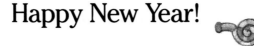

Take the old
calendar down . . .

. . . and hang up a
new one!

DECEMBER
31

JANUARY
1

At midnight on December 31st,
the old year ends,
and the New Year begins.

Hooray!

January

warm coats

wooly hats

cozy mittens

winter boots

long scarves

snuggly snowsuit

bulky sweater

heavy sweatshirt

thick socks

It's snowing outside!

Bundle, pull, struggle. Snuggle, wrap. Snap, snap, snap!

Snow

A snowflake begins . . .

                     . . . as a drop of water . . .

         . . . that falls from a cloud.

In the cold air . . .

                    . . . the water freezes . . .

               . . . and becomes a snowflake.

A Different Winter

In a warm climate, there is no snow.
During winter, it sometimes rains
and is breezy.

Flowers bloom outdoors and orange
trees grow fruit all winter long.

The farther north you live, the
longer winter is. The farther south
you live, the shorter winter is.

Groundhog Day

Legend says, if the groundhog comes out of his burrow and sees his shadow, there will be six more weeks of winter. If he does not see his shadow, there will be an early spring.

Shadow!

No shadow!

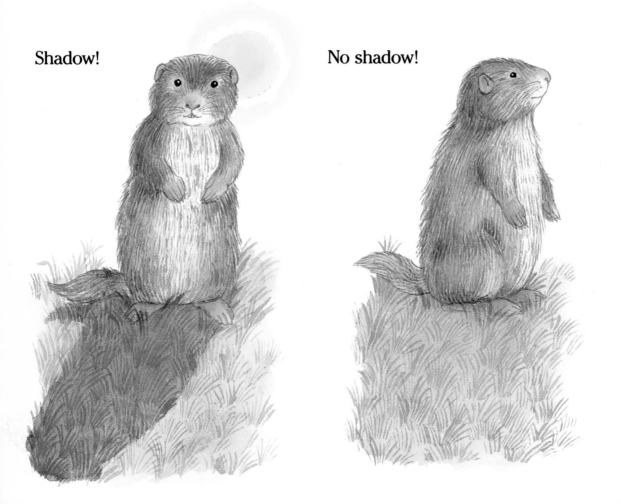

A Nature Hunt

When you see animal tracks, think about what animal has paws or feet that are like the tracks.

Where are the tracks? Tracks near a hedge may be made by a wild rabbit.

Look for other clues. A hole in the ground and broken nutshells may mean that a squirrel has dug up a nut.

Raccoon

Mouse

Bird

Deer

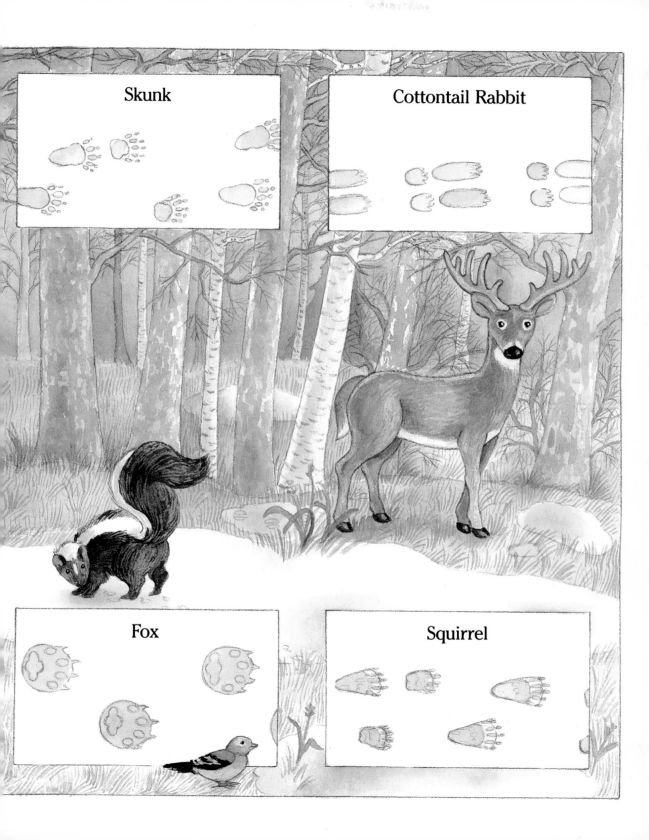

Skunk

Cottontail Rabbit

Fox

Squirrel

Valentine's Day

March

As winter ends, the earth moves closer to the sun. Days are warmer and longer.

Sap runs in trees again and leaf buds are plump, waiting to open.

Birds that flew south begin to return.

Underground, it seems that all is quiet, but daffodil and tulip bulbs are beginning to grow.